GALAXY ZACK

ZACK

HELLO, NEBULON!

By Ray O'Ryan

Illustrated by Colin Jack

LITTLE SIMON

New York   London   Toronto   Sydney   New Delhi

LITTLE SIMON
An imprint of Simon & Schuster Children's Publishing Division
1230 Avenue of the Americas, New York, New York 10020
Copyright © 2013 by Simon & Schuster, Inc.
All rights reserved, including the right of reproduction
in whole or in part in any form.
LITTLE SIMON is a registered trademark of Simon & Schuster, Inc., and
associated colophon is a trademark of Simon & Schuster, Inc.
For information about special discounts for bulk purchases, please
contact Simon & Schuster Special Sales at 1-866-506-1949
or business@simonandschuster.com.
The Simon & Schuster Speakers Bureau can bring authors to your
live event. For more information or to book an event contact
the Simon & Schuster Speakers Bureau at 1-866-248-3049
or visit our website at www.simonspeakers.com.
Designed by Nicholas Sciacca
Manufactured in the United States of America 0814 MTN
5 6 7 8 9 10
Library of Congress Cataloging-in-Publication Data
O´Ryan, Ray.
Hello, Nebulon! / by Ray O´Ryan ; illustrated by Colin Jack. — 1st ed.
p. cm. — (Galaxy Zack ; 1)
Summary: Moving from Earth to the futuristic planet Nebulon in 2120,
eight-year-old Zack is nervous about starting school and meeting
people.
ISBN 978-1-4424-5386-9 (pbk. : alk. paper) — ISBN 978-1-4424-5387-6
(hardcover : alk. paper) — ISBN 978-1-4424-5388-3 (ebook)
[1. Science fiction. 2. Moving, Household—Fiction. 3. Human-alien
encounters—Fiction. 4. Friendship—Fiction.] I. Jack, Colin, ill. II. Title.
PZ7.O7843He 2013
[Fic]—dc23
2011052777

CONTENTS

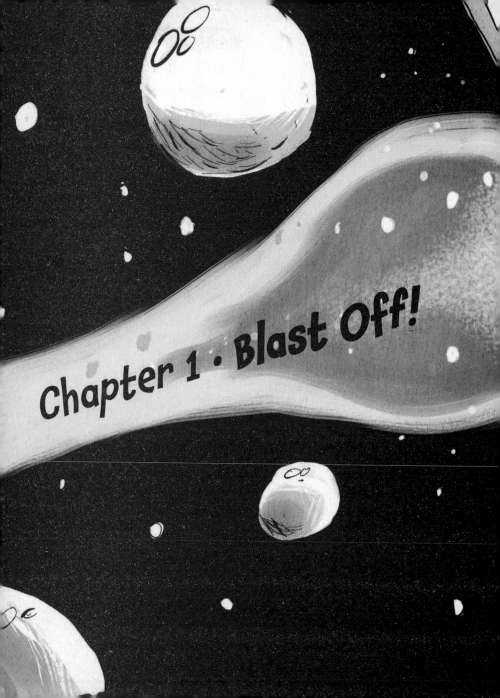

Chapter 1 · Blast Off!

"Ooh! Look, Zack," called Shelly Nelson from the front seat of the Nelson family's space cruiser. She pointed out of the large, round windshield in front of her. "It's Venus! And there's Mars!"

Sitting in the backseat of the

cruiser, eight-year-old Zack Nelson sighed. He knew his mom was just trying to cheer him up. But at the moment all he wanted to do was go home—to his real home, Earth. Not his new home on some planet called Nebulon.

Zack punched a code into the keypad below his window. The glass in the

window changed
from dark to clear.

Billions of stars
glittered in the inky
blackness beyond the
window. This was the
part of space travel Zack liked
best. Sure, he could see tons of
stars with his überzoom galactic
telescope back on Earth. But being out
among the stars and planets, seeing
them close up, always made Zack
happy.

Except today, February 11, 2120.
Moving day.

Glancing out his window, Zack looked past Venus and Mars. He had visited both planets many times. His family had often taken weekend trips to the Low Gravity Amusement Park on Venus. And they had always gone to the beaches at the Red Planet Resort on Mars for spring break.

But today all Zack could see was Earth. The tiny blue and white ball grew smaller and smaller in the window. The Nelsons' space cruiser zoomed farther away from the only home Zack had ever known.

Zack's dad, Otto, was up front in the pilot's seat, steering the cruiser.

"How ya doing back there, Captain?" he called.

Zack smiled. He was years away from getting his pilot's license, but his dad always called him "Captain" whenever the family took a space trip.

"I guess I'm okay," mumbled Zack.

"He's just sad because . . . ," began Charlotte.

". . . he's going to miss Bert . . . ," Cathy continued.

". . . and Luna," they said together.

Charlotte and Cathy Nelson were Zack's eleven-year-old identical twin sisters. They often spoke as if they were one person. They sat side by side in the seats next to Zack, finishing each other's sentences.

Zack's sisters had round faces with freckles. They both had flaming red hair like their father. Charlotte kept her hair in a ponytail. Cathy wore her hair in two braided pigtails. That was the only way most people could tell them apart.

"You'll still be able to talk to Bert, honey," Zack's mom said. Bert was Zack's best friend on Earth. "Between video chats and z-mail, it'll almost be like you never left."

"And Bert will take good care . . ."

". . . of Luna," said Charlotte and Cathy.

"You know that Bert . . ."

". . . loves dogs . . ."

9

". . . especially Luna," they added.

"The girls are right, Captain," said Dad. "Luna will join us as soon as we get settled on Nebulon. Then the whole family will be together again."

Zack just shrugged and stared out the window, watching Earth grow tinier by the second.

Chapter 2
Buggy Pizza!

"You'll love it on Nebulon, Captain," Dad said. "Wait'll you see the gadgets they have there. They're way ahead of Earth!"

"That sounds pretty cool," Zack said. Then he grew quiet. *Dad's got his great new job at Nebulonics, Zack* thought. *Mom wants to start her own business. And the twins always have each other. They don't have to worry about making new friends.*

Zack leaned back in his seat and closed his eyes.

"Okay, class, time for our Zerbanese language lesson," said someone with a strange, high-pitched voice.

Zack's eyes popped open. He was in a classroom on Nebulon. All his classmates looked like monsters. And slimy creatures with dripping tentacles

sat all around him. The teacher looked like a giant two-headed snake.

Zack dashed from the classroom and ran across the street. He hurried toward a huge sign that flashed the words: THIS GALAXY'S BEST PIZZA.

Zack loved pizza. "Ah, pizza," he said. It was his favorite food. "At least they have *something* that

I know on this wacky, crazy planet!"

Zack rushed into the pizza place and ordered a whole pie. "I'll have today's special pizza, please."

Soon a steaming pizza floated down.

"YAAA!" yelled Zack. The pizza was covered with slithering worms and crawling

insects. It was topped with extra-moldy

cheese.

Zack ran as fast as he could from

the pizza place. He pulled out his

video-chat hyperphone. Then he quickly entered Bert's z-mail address.

"Gotta talk to Bert," Zack mumbled to himself. "Maybe he can help me."

The screen on the hyperphone blinked. Then a message popped up: ERROR . . . CANNOT CONNECT TO EARTH.

"No!" cried Zack as he shoved the hyperphone back into his pocket. "I'm trapped here! And I'll never see or talk to my friends again!"

Zack felt a hand on his shoulder. Then he heard a familiar voice.

"Zack? Zack? Are you okay?"

Zack's eyes sprang open. He was looking up at his mom. They were still in the space cruiser, on their way to Nebulon.

"Bad dream, honey?" asked Mom, smoothing back Zack's thick blond hair.

"I guess so," Zack replied, rubbing his eyes.

A green light below the cruiser's front window began blinking. "Arrival on Nebulon in five minutes," said the cruiser's talking computer.

"This is so exciting!" Mom said as she sat back down in her seat. "Don't worry, Zack. This is going to be a great adventure!"

"Arriving on Nebulon in one minute. Please prepare for landing," said the cruiser's robotic voice.

"This is it, gang!" announced Dad. He was hardly able to contain his excitement.

Zack checked his safety belt. Then

he pressed his face to the window. His eyes opened wide as the planet below got closer and closer. Through thin pink clouds, Zack saw purple patches of land and large orange oceans. *Nebulon looks nothing like Earth,* he thought.

Chapter 3
Landing . . .
Landing . . .
Landed!

The space cruiser drifted down. Soon a busy spaceport came into view.

"What are those other cruisers, Dad?" Zack asked. He stared down at what looked like tiny flying spaceships. They zoomed around in the air.

"Oh, those are Nebulon cars,"

25

explained Dad. "On Nebulon, cars and trains glide through the air. No more bumps or potholes!"

"Landing . . . landing . . . landing . . . ," the computer repeated.

A few seconds later the Nelson's space cruiser touched down on Nebulon.

When they stepped outside, an

odd-looking man greeted them.
"Welcome to Nebulon, Otto Nelson
and Otto Nelson's family," he said.

Zack stared at the man. He was
slightly taller than Dad. His head
was egg-shaped, and his arms were
long and skinny. They dangled down
to his knees.

"Hi, Fred! Thanks for meeting us,"

said Dad. "Everyone, this is Fred Stevens, my new boss at Nebulonics."

Fred lifted his hand with his palm facing out. Then he moved his hand in a small circle in front of his face.

Zack looked at his sisters. "What is this guy doing?" he whispered.

Dad made the same movement with his hand. "That's how Nebulites shake hands," Dad explained. "Fred, this is my wife, Shelly."

Mom raised her hand and made a circle. "How do you do?" she said with a giggle.

"How do I do what?" Fred asked, looking very puzzled.

"That's how Earthlings say 'hello,'" Dad explained.

"Well then, how do you do?" asked
Fred.

"And these are my daughters,
Charlotte and Cathy," Dad continued.
"And my son, Zack."

"Nice to . . ."

". . . meet you . . ."

"... Mr. Stevens," the twins said.

"Hi," Zack added.

"It is time to choose a car and go to your new home," said Fred. The Nelsons followed him into the spaceport's main terminal.

They soon arrived at a big sign that simply read: CARS.

"We are here, Otto Nelson," said Fred. "I will leave you to choose a car. I will see you at the office tomorrow. Good-bye, Otto Nelson's family."

Fred Stevens left the spaceport.

Zack looked at the tall shelves under the CARS sign. Small boxes that came in hundreds of different colors floated in rows.

"Uh, Dad, I don't see any cars here,"
said Zack. "All I see are some box
things."

"Welcome to Nebulon, Zack," Dad
said. "Pick a color."

"Uh, okay . . . green, I guess," said
Zack.

"Green it is," Dad said. He reached up and pulled a green box from the shelf. "Watch this."

Dad pressed a button on the box. It instantly changed into the coolest car Zack had ever seen.

"Hop in, everyone!" Dad said. "It's all ours."

"Does this thing have a GPS, Dad?" Zack asked as he got into the car.

"Better than GPS, buddy," replied Dad. "Look."

Dad pressed a button on the dashboard. "One twenty-two Zoid View,

Creston City," he said. Then he leaned back and placed his hands behind his head.

"Calculating," said a voice from the dashboard.

Without warning, the car sped out of the spaceport and into traffic.

Chapter 4
What a House!

The Nelsons' car flew through the air above Nebulon.

"One twenty-two Zoid View directly below," said the car. It slowed down as it approached a large house.

The house was shiny white. The car glided softly into a big, rounded

garage. It parked next to a smaller red car.

"Destination reached," announced the car. Then the engine shut off.

"Well, Nelsons, we're home!" Dad announced. "Who wants a tour?"

"Me!" Charlotte shouted.

"And me!" Cathy agreed.

"Zack?" Dad asked.

"Uh . . . sure, I guess," Zack said, shrugging.

"Oh, I think you're really going to like this place, Zack," Dad said. "First stop—the kitchen."

Dad walked over to a round door in the garage. He went into a tiny room.

"*That's* the kitchen?" asked Zack.

"Nope. This is the elevator. Come on in, everyone."

The whole family stepped into the elevator. The door closed with a *whoosh*. The elevator took off—going sideways.

"The elevator connects all the sections of the house," explained Dad. "It travels through tubes. It goes up, down, forward, and backward."

The elevator glided to a stop, and the doors slid open.

Mom stepped into the huge kitchen. "Wow!" she said.

"Welcome home, Mr. Nelson," said a voice that seemed to be coming from every corner of the room.

"How ya doing, Ira?" Dad replied.

"Ira?" Mom asked. "Who's Ira?"

"Where's . . ."

". . . Ira?" asked the twins.

"*What's Ira?*" Zack asked.

"I-R-A is short for 'Indoor Robotic Assistant,'" Dad explained. "He's a computer, but he's so much more. Ira is part of the electrical, mechanical, computer, and communications

systems of every room in the house."

"Hi, Ira," said Zack, giggling a bit. *I'm talking to the house,* he thought.

"Welcome home, Master Zack," Ira replied.

And the house is talking to me!

"You don't have to call me 'Master Zack,'" said Zack. "Just 'Zack' is fine."

"Very well, Master Just Zack," Ira said.

The whole family chuckled.

"And welcome to you, too, Mrs. Nelson. Miss Charlotte. Miss Cathy."

"Ooh, I like . . ."

". . . being called . . ."

". . . 'miss'!" said the twins.

"So, who's thirsty after the long journey?" Dad asked.

"Can I have some orange juice?" asked Zack.

"Just plain old orange juice?" Dad smiled, and his eyes opened wide. "How about a jazzy Nebulon juice?"

"Sure, I guess," Zack said.

"Ira, can we please have a spudsy melonade?" said Dad.

"Certainly, Mr. Nelson," Ira said.

A small panel in the wall slid open.

Out popped a metal arm holding a glass of frosty, bubbling juice. "Here is your spudsy melonade, Master Just Zack," said Ira.

Zack looked at the glass with wide eyes. "Thanks, Ira," he said. Then Zack took it and gulped down the cool drink. "Sweet! Spudsy melonade rules!" *Maybe this place won't be so bad after all*, he thought.

Chapter 5
Wired!

"Why don't you kids check out your new bedrooms before dinner?" said Dad.

Zack and the twins stepped into the elevator. The door closed behind them and the elevator took off.

A moment later the elevator slowed

to a stop. The door slid open. Zack
stared into a large bedroom. It was
covered in pink. Frilly curtains hung
from the windows.

Zack shuddered. "Ugh! This is *your*

stop," he said to his sisters.

"Ooooh . . . ," said Cathy and Charlotte, running into the room.

The door zipped shut and the elevator sped off. A couple of seconds later it stopped, and the door opened again.

"Now, *this* is my room," said Zack, smiling. He stepped into the bedroom.

The walls were green. So were the carpet and curtains.

Most things in the room were green.
Green was Zack's favorite color.

Zack spotted a huge desk. A computer touchpad was built into the desktop. The entire wall in front of it was a giant view screen.

"That's awfully big for a computer monitor," Zack said. He touched the screen. Suddenly he was looking at a HELLO, ZACK message, then zillions of stars in space. "Wow! This is so cool!" he said. "I can see the whole galaxy!"

Zack searched the stars and planets around Nebulon for a few minutes.
Then he looked around the room.

"Hey," Zack said. "Where's my
bed?"

"Are you ready for bed,
Master Just Zack?" Ira
asked.

Zack jumped at
the sound of his
voice.

"Are you in here,
too, Ira?" Zack asked.

"I am wired throughout the house,"
Ira explained. "Here is your bed."

A panel in the ceiling opened and
a bed came down from above. The
bed had a pillow with a matching
green pillowcase and blanket.

"Cool!" Zack said. "Thanks, Ira. But
it's too early for bed."

"Very well," Ira said. The bed went back into the ceiling.

"You mean I don't have to make my bed every morning?" asked Zack. "Sweet!"

"Zack, honey," called Mom through the commu-link. "Dinnertime."

Zack scooted into the elevator and rode to the dining room. He took a seat at a table that floated in midair. Charlotte and Cathy sat across from him. Mom and Dad sat on either side.

"So, Mom, what's for dinner?" Zack asked. "Are we going out?"

"No need," said Dad. A big, cheery smile spread across his face. He turned to the twins. "Girls, what would you like for dinner?"

"Spaghetti!" they both shouted.

"You got it! Zack?"

"I want a pepperoni pizza," Zack replied.

"No problem," said Dad. "Your mother and I will have grilled salmon with baked potatoes."

"Where are we going to get all that, Dad?" Zack asked.

"Right here! Ira, two spaghetti dinners, one pepperoni pizza, and two plates of grilled salmon with baked potatoes."

"Right away, Mr. Nelson," said Ira.

"Ira cooks, too?" Zack wondered aloud.

A panel in the ceiling slid open. Five plates of steaming hot food floated down and landed on the table.

Zack pulled a slice of pizza from

the pie. It had crispy star-shaped pepperoni slices that floated on top of the
gooey cheese. As Zack took his first
bite he suddenly realized just how
hungry he was.

"Wow!" said Zack. "This pizza
is great. It tastes just like the
pizza at Tip-Top Pizza
back on Earth! You
know, I think living
on Nebulon might
not be that bad
after all."

"I'm so glad,
honey," Mom said.

"After dinner we can make sure that you and your sisters are all ready for tomorrow."

"Tomorrow?" Zack asked through a mouthful of pizza.

"Yes. We've registered you at Sprockets Academy," Mom explained. "Tomorrow you start school on Nebulon."

School! Zack thought. He stopped chewing his pizza. Zack remembered his nightmare about school, and his monster classmates and two-headed snake teacher. *I forgot all about school!*

Chapter 6

Ready?
Set?
School!

Zack went to bed after dinner. He tossed and turned for most of the night.

What if nobody at school likes me? he worried. *What if they think that people from Earth are weird? I wish Bert were here.*

After staring at the ceiling for hours,

Zack finally fell into a deep sleep.

The next morning a strangely familiar voice woke him up.

"Good morning, Master Just Zack. It
is time to get ready for school."

Zack sat upright in bed. "Ira, is that you?" he asked, rubbing the sleep from his eyes.

"Yes. It is six a.m. galactic standard time. You set the alarm for that time," Ira said.

"Yeah, but I didn't expect *you* to wake me up," Zack explained. "Back on Earth, my alarm clock played my favorite song to wake me up."

"What is your favorite song?" asked Ira.

"Oh, Ira, I don't think you'd know it," Zack said. "It's called 'Rockin' Round the Stars.' It's by an Earth band called—"

"Retro Rocket," Ira said. "It was released in 2117."

Suddenly the song came blasting into Zack's room.

"You know 'Rockin' Round the Stars'?" Zack cried.

"Certainly. My memory banks contain more than six million songs from twenty-three different planets."

"Cool. Can you wake me up with that song from now on?"

"Of course," Ira replied. "Now hurry. You will be late for school."

Zack rushed into the bathroom and stepped into the shower. "Now what?"

A blast of water startled Zack.

"YA!" cried Zack. "It's too cold!"

"Adjusting," said Ira.

The water quickly became just the right temperature.

"Shall I save that shower setting for you?" Ira asked.

"You do everything, don't you?"

"Yes, I do," replied Ira.

Zack got dressed and zoomed to the kitchen. He ate toast with boingoberry jam, which was made from a berry that grew on Venus.

"Okay, everybody, have a great day!" Dad said.

"Cathy and Charlotte will be in phase five," Mr. Spudnik explained. "And Zack will be in phase two. I will show you the way."

"Bye, kids!" Mom shouted as Zack and the twins followed Mr. Spudnik. "Have a great day!"

"I have an early meeting with Fred Stevens. I'll be driving the red Nebulonics car. Bye!"

After Dad left, Mom hurried Zack and the twins into the green car.

"Are you sure you know how to work this thing, Mom?" asked Zack.

"Dad showed me," Mom replied. "I just push this button and say 'Sprockets Academy.'"

As soon as she did that, the car zoomed into the air.

When they arrived at Sprockets Academy, a Nebulite man stepped

up to the car to greet them. "Welco to Sprockets Academy," he s "My name is Mr. Spudnik. I am principal."

"Nice to meet you," said Mom. "Th is Zack, Cathy, and Charlotte." Th three kids got out of the car.

They dropped off Charlotte and Cathy at their classroom. Then Mr. Spudnik and Zack reached Zack's classroom.

"Ms. Rudolph, this is Zack Nelson. His family just moved to Nebulon from Earth," Mr. Spudnik said. "Zack, this is your teacher, Ms. Rudolph."

"Welcome, Zack," Ms. Rudolph said. "You know, I'm from Earth too."

"You are?" Zack asked.

"I moved to Nebulon about a year ago," Ms. Rudolph explained. "At first I missed Earth terribly. But now I can't imagine living anywhere but Nebulon. I think in time you'll feel the same way."

Zack found a seat and sat down. *Ms. Rudolph seems really nice, Zack* thought. *And Nebulites speak English. That'll make things a little easier.*

"Class, I would like you all to meet Zack Nelson," Ms. Rudolph said.

The students turned to face Zack. Every eye in the room was staring right at him.

Chapter 7
Yippee Wah-Wah!

"Hi!" said Zack. Then he raised his hand and moved it in a circle—just like his dad had done at the spaceport. The other students just stared.

"Okay, class, let's begin with today's history lesson," Ms. Rudolph said. She sat and then began typing.

Zack stared at the small screen in front of him.

How do I get this thing to work? he wondered.

A Nebulite boy sitting next to Zack leaned over. "Just tap the center of the screen," the boy whispered.

"Thanks," Zack whispered back. He tapped his screen and the lesson appeared.

Zack enjoyed learning about the history of Nebulon.

After history they studied math and science.

Then the bell rang for lunch, and everyone dashed from the classroom.

The students boarded a space bus to take them from the classroom to the cafeteria.

SPROCKETS

Zack stepped onto the bus. He saw kids talking and laughing. Zack felt like he was all alone.

What I am doing here? he thought. *I want to go home.*

"Hey, Zack. There is a seat over here," someone called out.

Zack looked toward the back of the

bus. He saw the Nebulite boy who sat next to him in class. Zack hurried down the aisle and sat next to the boy.

"I am Drake Taylor," the boy said, raising his hand and moving it in a circle.

"Nice to meet you," Zack said, doing the same hand movement.

The bus zoomed off from its dock outside the classroom building.

"How long has your family been living on Nebulon, Zack?" asked Drake.

Zack looked down at his Galactic Standard watch. "Hmm . . . about eighteen hours," Zack replied, smiling.

"How do you like it so far?" Drake asked.

"Parts of it are cool," said Zack. The last thing Zack wanted to do was to tell Drake how much he missed home.

The space bus slowed to a stop. The doors slid open, and everyone ran into the cafeteria.

Zack took a seat next to Drake and looked around.

"Hey—where's the lunch line?" Zack asked. "Where's all the food?"

"You will see," Drake replied.

Just then a line of robots came marching through the door. They were tall, skinny, and metal. Each of them pushed a cart filled with food.

A robot walked over to Zack and Drake. Zack read the choices. "I'll have super mac and cheese," he said.

The robot picked up a steaming plate of food. It set the plate down right in front of Zack.

"And I will have the jammin' jelly sandwich, please," Drake said. After Drake got his food, the boys began to eat.

"So, Zack, what did you do for fun on Earth?"

"I really liked going bike riding with my friend Bert," Zack replied.

"I, too, like to ride my bike," Drake said. "Maybe we could ride our bikes together."

"Yeah . . . okay," Zack said.

"How about we ride together today after school?" Drake asked.

"Um . . . all right."

When lunch was over, the space bus arrived to take everyone back to class. Zack and Drake took their seats.

"Yippee wah-wah," Drake said. "My favorite class is next."

Zack stared at his new friend. "I have two questions, Drake," said Zack. "What's your favorite class? And what does 'yippee wah-wah' mean?"

Drake laughed. Zack started laughing too.

"Planetology is my favorite class," Drake replied. "And 'yippee wah-wah' is what

Nebulite kids say when they are happy."

"I love studying planets and stars too," said Zack. He was happy that he met Drake. *Looks like I made a new friend*, he thought.

Chapter 8
Zoom! Zoom!

The rest of Zack's school day flew right by. He really liked planetology. He learned about planets and stars he had never even heard of on Earth.

When school was over, Zack's mom arrived to pick him up. Zack walked over to the car with Drake. Charlotte

95

and Cathy were already inside.

"Mom, this is my new friend, Drake," Zack said.

"Hello, Drake," Mom said. "Very nice to meet you."

"And these are my sisters, Charlotte and Cathy," Zack said.

"Hello," Drake said.

"Hi . . ."

". . . Drake. . . ."

"Nice to . . ."

". . . meet you," the twins said.

"Do they talk like that all the time?"
Drake whispered.

"All the time," Zack whispered back.

Zack got into the car. "Drake's coming over later to go bike riding," he said.

"That sounds like fun," Mom said. "We'll see you later, Drake."

Z

"We're home!" Mom announced as the car pulled into the garage.

Zack was so excited about going bike riding. He jumped out of the car and pulled his bike out from a corner of the garage.

As he got onto his bike, Zack saw something speeding toward the house.

"That looks like Drake, but what's he riding?" Zack wondered aloud.

Drake rode up to Zack. He was riding a bike.

But Zack had never seen a bike like this one. Drake's bike flew just above the ground, and it went faster than any bike Zack had ever ridden.

"Wow!" Zack cried. "What kind of bike is that?"

Drake looked puzzled. "It is just a regular Nebulon bike," he said. "Wow, you have a really old bike, Zack."

"No, it's not old,"

Zack said. "I got it for my birthday last year."

Drake just shrugged. "Come on. Time to ride."

Drake sped off on his bike. Zack pedaled hard. He tried to keep up, but his bike was not fast enough. Drake saw how far behind Zack was and hurried back.

"Would you like to try my bike?" Drake asked.

"Sure!" Zack said.

Zack climbed onto Drake's bike. It felt just like a regular bike.

"Just hold on tight and press that button on the handlebars," explained Drake. "I will ride your bike."

Zack pressed the button. He sped along just above the ground.

"This is so cool!" Zack shouted. "I have to get one of these!"

Zack looked back and saw Drake. He was pedaling Zack's bike and smiling. Drake was far away, so Zack turned around and rode back to his friend. As they rode back to the house, Zack daydreamed about zooming around on his own Nebulon bike.

Chapter 9
Surprise!

Dad arrived home as Zack pulled up in front of the house. Dad reached into the back of the car and took out a big box with a bright green bow.

"Have I got a surprise for you, buddy," said Dad.

"Hi, Dad. This is my friend Drake."

"Hello, Drake. I think you'll like this too," Dad said.

Maybe Dad got me a Nebulon bike! thought Zack.

But then Zack heard barking from inside the box. He quickly pulled the lid off. Out jumped Zack's dog, Luna.

"Luna!" Zack shouted. "I didn't think I'd see you so soon!"

Dad smiled. "I knew how much

you missed her, so I put Luna on the
next cruiser to Nebulon."

"Thanks, Dad," said Zack.

Luna jumped on Zack and licked his
face. Then she jumped up on Drake.
She almost knocked him over.

"What is THAT?" Drake cried, backing away.

"Don't be scared," Zack said. "It's just my dog, Luna. She's very friendly. Do you have a dog?"

"I have never seen a real dog before," Drake explained.

"Don't they have any dogs on Nebulon?" asked Zack.

"No," said Drake. "I think I saw a picture once, in a book."

"Well, here's something else they
don't have on Nebulon," Dad said. He
reached into the big box and pulled
out two candy bars.

"Chocolate Nutty Crunchy Gooey
Bars!" Zack said. "My favorite!"

Dad handed one candy bar to Zack and one to Drake. Both boys started munching on the treat.

"Yumzers!" Drake cried.

Zack laughed.

"That's what we say on Nebulon when something tastes really, really, really good!" explained Drake.

"Yumzers!" Zack repeated.

At that moment Mom, Charlotte, and Cathy joined the others outside.

"It's official," Mom announced. "I've decided to open a boutique. I'm going to sell Earth clothing to the women of Nebulon."

"Great idea, honey," Dad said.

"Yay!" Charlotte and Cathy both cheered.

Then Zack's hyperphone began to buzz. He pulled it from his pocket.

"Hi, Bert!" Zack said when the video chat connected. Bert's face popped up on the small screen. "Thanks for watching Luna. She just got here."

"Cool," Bert said. "I wanted to make sure she got there okay."

"How's life back on Earth?" Zack asked.

"Pretty good," Bert replied. "The Explorers Club went on a field trip to Calypso. It was fun."

"That's so cool! I hope my new school has an Explorers Club too," Zack said.

"Do you like living on Nebulon?" Bert asked.

Zack looked at his family. Then he looked at Drake and smiled. "I miss Earth," he said to Bert. "But I think I'm going to like living on Nebulon."

CHECK OUT THE NEXT

ADVENTURE!
HERE'S A SNEAK PEEK!

Zack stood in front of Sprockets Academy. He wore his Sprockets Explorers Club T-shirt. Today he was going to Juno!

The rest of the club was gathered outside the school. Zack spotted Seth Stevens. Seth was the last person Zack hoped would be on this trip. Then he saw Drake.

"Drake, over here!" Zack called. Drake joined him.

"I cannot believe we are really going to Juno," said Drake. "Only a handful of people have ever seen it."

A man stepped to the front of the crowd. He was tall and had a skinny green head. He had six long fingers on each hand.

On top of his head was a galactic blast cap that read DREXEL EXPLORERS CLUB. EARTH JOURNEY 2098. Clearly this man was neither a Nebulite nor a human.

"Welcome, explorers!" he began. "I am Mr. Shecky, the adviser of the Sprockets Explorers Club. I'll be your leader on your journey to Juno. Now please follow me onto the space cruiser."

Zack, Drake, and the rest of the explorers piled onto a small space cruiser. Mr. Shecky sat next to Zack.

A few moments later they took off into space.

Zack stared out the window and saw stars and comets streaking by.

A short while later the cruiser began beeping. Everyone leaned forward.

"Attention, please. Arrival on Juno in five minutes. Prepare for landing," the cruiser said.

Zack looked out the window. He saw a craggy-looking planet that sparkled. Juno looked as if it were covered in diamonds.

This is it! Zack thought.

The cruiser landed gently on the surface of Juno. The hatch opened and everyone stepped out. A sparkling crystal landscape stretched out before them.

Zack saw lots of space cruisers from other schools. They came from different planets, such as Zorba, Neptune, Cylon, and more.

Then Zack spotted the Nebulon Navigators team. They were already hard at work gathering samples.

"Wow! I can't believe I'm here with the Nebulon Navigators," Zack said to Drake.

"I'm going to break you into teams," said Mr. Shecky. "Everyone will work with a partner."

I hope Drake and I can be partners! thought Zack.

"You are to take notes, gather samples, and shoot video and photos with your team's handheld camtrams," Mr. Shecky continued.

Mr. Shecky began reading aloud pairs of names. When he got to Zack's name, Zack held his breath.

"'Zack Nelson and Seth Stevens!'" Mr. Shecky called out.

Oh no! Zack thought. *Not him!* He had a sinking feeling in the pit of his stomach.